Librarian Reviewer
Laurie K. Holland
Media Specialist (National Board Certified), Edina, MN
MA in Elementary Education, Minnesota State University, Mankato, MN

Reading Consultant
Elizabeth Stedem
Educator/Consultant, Colorado Springs, CO
MA in Elementary Education, University of Denver, CO

Graphic Sparks are published by Stone Arch Books,
A Capstone Imprint
1710 Roe Crest Drive
North Mankato, Minnesota 56003
www.capstonepub.com

Library of Congress Cataloging-in-Publication Data
Nickel, Scott.
 Night of the Homework Zombies / by Scott Nickel; illustrated by Steve Harpster.
 p. cm. — (Graphic Sparks. School Zombies)
 ISBN-13: 978-1-59889-035-8 (library binding)
 ISBN-10: 1-59889-035-2 (library binding)
 ISBN-13: 978-1-59889-172-0 (paperback)
 ISBN-10: 1-59889-172-3 (paperback)
 1. Graphic novels. I. Harpster, Steve. II. Title. III. Series.
PN6727.N544N54 2005
741.5—dc22   2005026687

Summary: Mr. Winklepoof, the new substitute teacher, is really a mad scientist. His
goal: turn every kid in school into a brain-boggled zombie who loves homework! "Study!
Study!" they chant. Only Trevor knows the truth. And only Trevor can save his friends, and
himself, from this truly horrible fate!

Art Director: Heather Kindseth
Production Manager: Sharon Reid
Production/Design: James Liebman, Mie Tsuchida
Production Assistance: Bob Horvath, Eric Murray

Printed in China
082011
006354R

NIGHT OF THE HOMEWORK ZOMBIES

BY SCOTT NICKEL

ILLUSTRATED BY STEVE HARPSTER

◤◥ STONE ARCH BOOKS

Minneapolis   San Diego

CAST OF CHARACTERS

MR. WINKLEPOOF

?

DR. BRAINIUM

TREVOR WALTON

19

ABOUT THE AUTHOR

Scott Nickel has written children's books, short fiction for *Boys' Life Magazine*, humorous greeting cards, and lots of really funny knock-knock jokes. Scott is also the author of many Garfield books.

Currently, Scott lives in Indiana with his wife, two sons, four cats, a parakeet, and several sea monkeys.

ABOUT THE ILLUSTRATOR

Steve Harpster has loved to draw funny cartoons, mean monsters, and goofy gadgets since he was able to pick up a pencil. In first grade, he was able to avoid his writing assignments by working on the pictures for stories instead.

Steve was able to land a job drawing funny pictures for books, and that's really what he's best at. Steve lives in Columbus, Ohio, with his wonderful wife, Karen, and their sheepdog, Doodle.

GLOSSARY

brainwash (BRAYN-wash) to make people act, or think, in a new way without them knowing it; the brain is "washed clean" of its old way of thinking.

contagious (kun-TAY-juhss) something that can spread from one person to another; a sickness can be contagious, or becoming a zombie, but boy-germs and girl-germs are not contagious.

mindless (MYND-liss) an activity is mindless if you don't have to use your brain while you're doing it; watching TV is mindless, but reading a graphic novel is not!

substitute (SUHB-stuh-toot) someone who takes another person's place, such as a substitute teacher or a substitute quarterback in a football game

zombie (ZOM-bee) someone whose brain is controlled by another person; when you tell your friend to eat worms, and he does it, he is acting like a zombie

zombify (ZOM-buh-fye) to turn someone into a zombie

Heh-heh-heh.
If you learn these words
your brain will get bigger.
And BIGGER!!

ZOMBIOLOGY

Are zombies real?

Some people think so. On the islands of the Caribbean, some people practice a religion known as Voudon, or voodoo. Voodoo beliefs say that a dead body can come back to life. A spirit, called a zombi, enters the dead body and gives it the power to move.

Zombie! Zombie! I want to be a zombie!

What does a zombie look like?

Zombies do not eat or drink. They move stiffly, have blank faces, and cannot speak. Real people who act like this, maybe a grown-up after a hard day at the office, are sometimes called zombies.

According to voodoo, zombies are under the control of the person who brought them back to life. Some scientists think that people given powerful drugs can behave like zombies. The drugs weaken their minds so that they will easily obey another person.

Computers can also be zombies. A zombie computer is one that is remotely controlled by another person in secret.

The famous writer Zora Neale Hurston met people on the island of Haiti who claimed to have seen a real zombie. A woman who had been buried 30 years earlier was walking the streets of a village. Later, Hurston found out that this was just a rumor.

DISCUSSION QUESTIONS

1.) Dr. Brainium brainwashes students so they will love homework. Homework is supposed to be good for you. So is it all right to be brainwashed into doing it?

2.) Trevor uses his own brainpower to come up with a plan to defeat Dr. Brainium. Who do you think is smarter, and why?

3.) Bo is saved from Dr. Brainium's evil scheme by his best friend Trevor. Trevor had to force Bo into watching cartoons and eating ice cream and cheese puffs. Is Trevor just as guilty of brainwashing as Dr. Brainium?

WRITING PROMPTS

1.) If you were Doctor Brainium and could brainwash other people into obeying your commands, what would you make them do, and why?

2.) Trevor is the only kid who escapes the brainwashing video because he was wasting time in the boys' bathroom. Write a story about what would happen if Trevor had stayed in the classroom along with everyone else. Would the students stay brainwashed forever?

3.) At the end of the story, the evil scientist is punished by having to work at Cheesy Charlie's Pizza Arcade. Write a story about what might happen if you went to a pizza place and met a mad scientist.

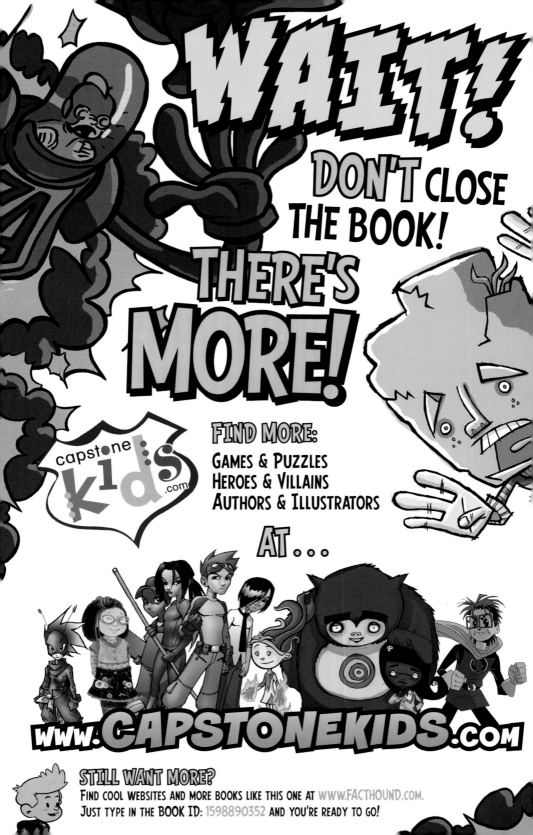